P9-CDJ-948

An Egg Is An Egg

written and illustrated by

NICKI WEISS

Macmillan McGraw-Hill

New York   Farmington

Macmillan/McGraw-Hill

A Division of The McGraw-Hill Companies

Copyright © 1997 Macmillan/McGraw-Hill, a Division of the Educational
and Professional Publishing Group of The McGraw-Hill Companies, Inc.

All rights reserved. No part of this book may be reproduced or
transmitted in any form or by any means, electronic or mechanical,
including photocopying, recording, or by any information storage and
retrieval system, without permission in writing from the publisher.

The publisher gratefully acknowledges permission to reprint
AN EGG IS AN EGG by Nicki Weiss.

AN EGG IS EGG by Nicki Weiss, copyright © 1990 by Monica J. Weiss.
Reprinted by permission of G. P. Putnam's Sons, a division of
The Putnam & Grosset Group, 200 Madison Avenue, New York, NY 10016.
Published simultaneously in Canada. Book design by
Golda Laurens.

Macmillan/McGraw-Hill
1221 Avenue of the Americas
New York, New York 10020

Printed in the United States of America

ISBN 0-02-181109-1 / 1, L. 3

5 6 7 8 9 FED 02 01 00 99 98

For Rachel

An egg is an egg
Until it hatches.

And then it is a chick.

A branch is a branch
Until it breaks.

And then it is a stick.

Nothing stays the same.
Everything can change.

A seed is a seed
Until it is sown.

And then it is a flower.

A block is a block
Until there are many.

And then they become a tower.

Nothing stays the same.
Everything can change.

Water is water
Until it is brewed.

And then it becomes tea.

You are you
Until I come.

And then you become "we."

Nothing stays the same.
Everything can change.

The yard is green
Until it snows.

And then it becomes white.

Day is day
Until sunset.

And then it is the night.

Nothing stays the same.
Everything can change.

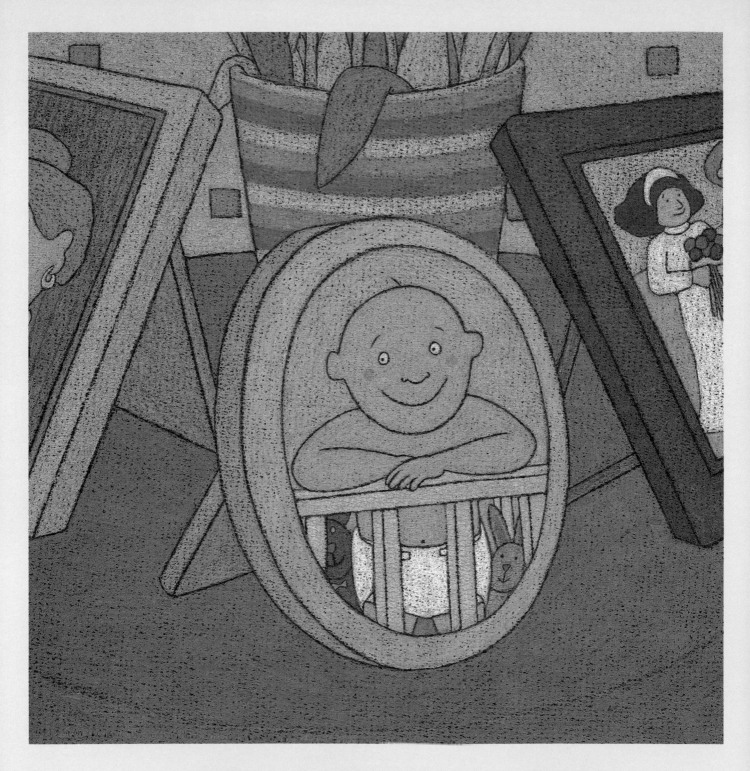

This baby was a baby
Until he grew.

And now he is a boy.

But you can always be a baby.

You will always be my baby.....

Some things stay the same.
Some things never change.